A SUMMER WITCHING

'Don't touch it, Ellen!' warned Beans. 'It might have a disease!'

Ellen seemed to have gone deaf. She crossed the clearing until she was a metre away from the cat and then stood still.

'My sweetling!' she said in a peculiar sing-song voice. 'My pigsnie!'

And the world jumped.

That was how it started – but Beans could never have guessed where that moment would lead her . . .

Thriller Firsts is an exciting series of fast-paced stories especially for younger readers of the seven to nine year age group. With clear, straightforward text and plenty of illustrations, readers are sure to be gripped.

Andrew Matthews was born in Barry, Glamorgan but now lives in Reading, Berkshire with his wife, Sheena, and their three cats. He has had four novels for children published and *A Summer Witching* is his first for Blackie.

Other titles in the series

THRILLER FIRSTS

A SUMMER WITCHING

Andrew Matthews

Illustrated by Beryl Sanders

Blackie

For Zoe the Brave
and
for Poogy, Spooky and Fifi

Copyright © 1989 Andrew Matthews
Illustrations © 1989 Beryl Sanders
First published 1989 by Blackie and Son Ltd

British Library Cataloguing in Publication Data

Matthews, Andrew, *1948-*
A summer witching
I. Title
823'.914 [F]

ISBN 0-216-92752-8

Blackie and Son Ltd
7 Leicester Place
London WC2H 7BP

Typeset by Jamesway Graphics

Printed in Great Britain

1

Dead Man's Wood

Beans had been looking forward to the Sunday picnic since the start of the summer holidays. She had helped Mum and Dad prepare the food and they had let her invite Ellen, her best friend. Beans had chosen Cold Harbour Bay because it was her favourite place and because it was perfect for a picnic: the beach was pebbled, which meant no sand in the food, and if she got fed up with looking at the sea, she could always go for a walk in the nearby woods.

Unfortunately, that Sunday was hot and the beach was packed with holiday-makers. The blare of their portable radios and the smell of their sun-tan lotion filled the air. It took half an hour to find a space, and by that time the sandwiches had gone soggy and the canned drinks had turned to warm foam.

'It's not fair!' grumbled Beans, pushing a lick of sweaty hair off her forehead. 'We live here!'

'Don't be selfish, Beans!' said Ellen. 'In winter, when it's freezing cold and pouring with rain, we get the place all to ourselves!' She stuck out her bottom lip and tried to blow a draught over her face. 'Now I know what a beefburger feels like when it's being micro-waved!' she said. 'Any minute a bell's going to go ping and a huge hand is going to stick me inside a bun!'

Dad looked up from his newspaper and laughed. Mum, lying on her back trying to get a tan, smiled.

'Every time I want to do something, it gets spoiled!' moaned Beans.

'Ellen,' said Dad, 'why don't you take Robina for a walk and cheer her up? I think she's getting a blonk on.'

'I have not got a blonk on!' snapped Beans.

'Maybe not a king-sized one,' said Dad, 'but a blonkette, at any rate.'

Ellen stood up and smoothed the baggy knees out of her jeans.

'Come on, Beans!' she said. 'Let's go get an ice-cream or something!'

Beans clambered to her feet with a sigh;

Dad was right about her mood, though she would never have admitted it.

Dad held out a pound coin.

'Ice-creams are on me,' he said. 'But just one thing before you go, Ellen. Why do you call Robina "Beans"?'

'Because everyone else at school calls her "Ribena",' Ellen explained.

'Yes . . .' murmured Dad, frowning, 'of course . . . It's obvious, really . . .'

Beyond the sea wall, a tarmac path ran through a meadow, over a little stream and then broadened out into a car-park. The meadow was as crowded as the beach. To the left of the path, a pack of teenaged boys was being loud in the crazy-golf course. At the edge of the car-park, a long line of people queued up outside the ice-cream kiosk.

'We'll be standing in that queue for hours!' complained Beans as she stumped up the path beside Ellen. The tarmac had gone so soft in the sun that it was like walking over a freshly-chewed toffee.

'I'm not sure I really fancy one,' said Ellen.

'Ice-cream's gone a bit weird recently. They've got one now called a Slime Beast Special! Who wants to eat an ice cream with a name like that!'

Beans, who *had* eaten a Slime Beast Special, blushed. 'You can talk! You used to eat dog biscuits!'

'Dog biscuits are all right!' said Ellen. 'Especially the yellow ones. Anyway, that was last year, when I was having my dog craze. I wanted to know what it felt like to be a dog.'

'I'm surprised you didn't try peeing over a lamppost!'

'Lady dogs don't pee over lampposts,' Ellen pointed out. 'They sort of coopie down and –'

'Ell-en!' exclaimed Beans. 'I've only just eaten! Can we talk about something else?'

Ellen stopped walking and smiled.

'I've got an idea!' she said. 'I know where we can go to get away from everyone!'

'Where?' asked Beans.

'Dead Man's Wood.'

'Dead Man's Wood?' hooted Beans. 'No one ever goes into Dead Man's Wood!'

'Exactly!' beamed Ellen. 'The perfect place

for a quiet stroll!'

'But it's creepy!'

'The perfect place for a quiet, creepy stroll, then,' Ellen said happily. 'What's the matter, Beans? Are you chicken?'

Beans frowned unhappily. No one ever said, 'Don't go into Dead Man's Wood' like they said 'Don't talk to strangers', but they told eerie stories about it. Its proper name was 'Holden's Farm Wood', but nobody ever called it that.

Ellen made clucking noises and strutted like a hen. Passers-by gave her funny looks.

'OK!' said Beans. 'But I'm not staying long!'

They walked through the car-park and followed the footpath until they reached the stile that led to Dead Man's Wood. Ellen straddled the stile and wiggled her eyebrows.

'An adventure into the unknown!' she said in her horror-film voice.

'Are you going to spend the whole afternoon winding me up?' sighed Beans.

Ellen wiggled her eyebrows again and smiled broadly.

2

A Ginger Cat

On the far side of the stile, the path ran into the trees beside a small stream. Beans blinked nervously at the cool shadows, but it all looked the same as every other wood she had been in.

'There's supposed to be wild cats in here,' said Ellen.

'Wild cats?' yelped Beans, her head full of panthers.

'Ordinary cats that have gone wild,' Ellen explained patiently. 'I hope we see some!'

'What do they eat?'

'Tins of cat food,' said Ellen sarcastically. 'They burgle the local Spar at night!'

'No need to get huffy!' said Beans. 'I was thinking out loud.' She nodded at the trees. 'Looks ordinary, doesn't it?'

'What were you expecting?' laughed Ellen. 'Goblins dancing in a ring?'

'Vampire bats,' blurted Beans. She regretted her words at once, knowing that Ellen would poke fun.

'Vampire bats?'

'It was a story Grandad used to tell,' said Beans. 'There was a farm here a long time ago, run by a man called Holden. He threw an old lady out of her cottage because he wanted more land. She cursed him and he just laughed in her face. Anyway, not long after, his cows started getting thin and they wouldn't give any milk. One night, he noticed a flock of bats coming out of the wood. They landed on his cows and sucked blood out of their necks. He went into the wood to find their nest, but they got him first. That's how it got the name Dead Man's Wood.'

Ellen waved her hands at a cloud of midges that had gathered around her head. 'They're small, but they're vampire-ish!' she said. 'Let's get away from the stream!'

They took a fork in the footpath that led deeper into the wood. The clammy air and the heavy, listening quiet made Beans feel uneasy. She was about to suggest turning back, when Ellen let out an excited whoop and ran ahead into a grassy clearing.

The grass was littered with broken stones

and part of a wall, crumbling and covered with brambles. Just beyond the wall, an overgrown rose bush was all that remained of a garden. The blossoms on the bush were white, but blotched with brown patches.

'The ruins of Holden's Farm!' Ellen announced confidently. 'Come on, bats! Grub up!'

'Stop mucking around!' frowned Beans.

'Hey, Beans, when the last drop of blood gets sucked out of you, do you reckon it makes the same noise as a straw at the bottom of a Coke bottle?'

'Oh, let's go back to the beach!' pleaded Beans. 'It's boring here! It's nothing but a lot of old stones!'

She was fibbing – something about the ruin disturbed her. It felt wrong to be there, like the feeling she got when Dad parked the car on double yellow lines.

'Ell–,' she began, then stopped as Ellen held her hand up for quiet and pointed.

Beans turned slowly.

On the far side of the clearing sat a big ginger cat, staring at them with half-closed green eyes. It was the mangiest-looking beast Beans had ever seen; its coat was grey with grime.

'Isn't it beautiful?' breathed Ellen.

At first, Beans thought Ellen must be joking, but when she looked in Ellen's face she saw that her friend was perfectly serious.

Ellen held out her hand and took two careful steps forward.

'Don't touch it, Ellen!' warned Beans. 'It might have a disease!'

Ellen seemed to have gone deaf. She crossed the clearing until she was a metre away from the cat and then stood still.

'My sweetling!' she said in a peculiar sing-song voice. 'My pigsnie!'

And the world jumped.

It was like the kick Beans sometimes did when she was falling asleep, or the bright flick of a flash-gun and it made her catch her breath. For an instant, the clearing changed – the ruin was no longer a ruin and the ginger cat was something else – but before Beans could be certain what had happened, the change vanished like a star from a sparkler.

Ellen bent down slowly to pick up a stone from the grass. To Beans' horror, she flung the stone straight at the ginger cat. The cat yowled and rocketed off between the trees. Ellen turned and laughed unpleasantly.

'See it go?'

'What did you do that for?' gasped Beans.

'It was dirty!' spat Ellen. 'Someone ought to put down some poisoned meat and get rid of the whole filthy lot!'

Beans could hardly believe what she heard. Ellen was so soft about animals that she

wouldn't squash spiders, even though she hated them.

'But that's cruel!' Beans protested.

'Cats are vermin,' Ellen said coldly. 'They ought to be destroyed!'

She walked towards Beans, smiling; but the smile made Beans shudder; it might have been painted on. Above the smile, Ellen's eyes were sly.

'Are you all right?' Beans asked.

'Why shouldn't I be?'

'You seem a bit–'

'Let's get back to the beach,' Ellen interrupted. 'You're right, this place is boring!'

When they rejoined Mum and Dad, Ellen went into a stream of silly jokes about the way the holiday-makers were behaving, but she said nothing about Dead Man's Wood. Every time Beans tried to say something, Ellen interrupted her and gave her a strange, angry look.

Beans remembered how her best friend at school used to be Alice Arren. One day, for no reason Beans could explain, Alice had turned against her and told nasty lies about her. She wondered if the same thing might be happening with Ellen.

But when Dad stopped the car outside her house, Ellen smiled at Beans and said, 'I did have fun today, Robina. Will you come and see me tomorrow afternoon?'

'Yes, all right.'

Ellen turned to Mum and Dad.

'Thank you ever so much, Mr and Mrs Deeping!' she gushed. 'It was so kind of you to invite me!'

When Ellen had given a final wave from outside her front door, Mum said, 'What did Ellen just call you?'

'Robina.'

'I thought she called you Beans?'

Beans shrugged. 'Ellen calls people all sorts of things.'

3

Sour Milk

Beans woke up. At first, she thought that something in a dream had woken her, but when she tried to remember the dream, it slipped away. The luminous dial of the clock on the bedside table read 00:17. Beans didn't know if that meant late Sunday night or early Monday morning.

There was a faint, high sound. Beans lay still, trying to identify it. The house was old, and often talked to itself at night in a strange language of gurgling pipes and creaking boards. Beans knew every noise and this was different. It was coming from outside, a sad sound that pulsed like the beam of a lighthouse.

Beans decided to ignore it, snuggled deeper under the warm duvet and tried to make sleep come back. The sound wouldn't be ignored, it nagged at her until she knew that she wouldn't be able to doze off unless she discovered what was causing it.

Beans knelt up in bed and pushed her head and shoulders under the curtains of the bedroom window. It was a clear night. The moon was bright enough to cast shadows in the back garden. The garden went uphill in three steps: a patio, a small lawn edged with rose bushes and then a vegetable garden with a little shed at the end.

Beans saw something come down off the garden wall and pad across the patio. It was a cat, mewing for all it was worth. Beans didn't know whether it was upset or celebrating. The cat paced to the edge of the patio, turned round on itself and paced back. Back and forth it went, calling and calling.

It was strange, but the cat reminded Beans of the one she had seen in Dead Man's Wood with Ellen. For a second, she would have sworn it was the same; then she was not so sure. The cat in the garden looked ginger, but it was difficult to be certain in the moonlight. Anyway, it would have to have travelled miles to get to her house from the woods.

Beans felt a wave of sleep rise through her. The cat would be all right, she told herself. Cats could take care of themselves. She slid out from under the curtain, down under the duvet and went back to sleep as soon as her head touched the pillow.

Beans slept in later than usual and by the time she got downstairs next morning, Dad had already left for work and Mum was loading breakfast dishes into the dish-washer.

'Hello, thing,' Mum said. 'Sleep all right?'

'I got woken up in the night by a cat crying in the garden.'

'Lucky you,' said Mum. 'Your father woke me up with his famous snore! Fancy a poached egg?'

'No,' said Beans. 'It's like eating a yellow eye. I'll make myself some toast.'

Beans took her favourite mug (with a picture of a hippo in a dress on it) out of the cupboard and filled it with tea from the pot. As she poured milk into the tea, she pulled a face. Yellow lumps floated on the surface of the tea.

'Yee-ukk!'

'What's up?' Mum asked.

'The milk's off!'

'It was all right just now when I used it,' said Mum, frowning. She picked up the milk jug, sniffed it and pulled a face.

'Ugh! You're right! Have to be dried stuff, I'm afraid.'

Mum reached a tin down from a cupboard and levered off the lid with a spoon handle. The tin's paper seal was unbroken.

'Can I pop it?' Beans asked eagerly. 'I love popping those things!'

'So do I,' said Mum regretfully. 'But then,

I've had my life, I suppose. Go on then!'

Beans smiled at the smooth white paper.

'You're gloating!' Mum exclaimed. 'I forbid you to gloat when I can't pop!'

Beans drove her finger down through the seal, pulled it back to make a long tear, then squealed in alarm.

Inside the tin, the milk powder was moving as dozens of small, shiny black creatures burrowed into it to escape the light.

'Mu-um!' wailed Beans.

Mum glanced into the tin and wriggled with disgust.

'Weevils!' she hissed. She hastily clattered the lid back on and dropped the tin into the pedal bin. 'I wonder how they got in there? They ought to take up burglary!' She noticed Beans looking glumly at her mug and smiled. 'I'll put the kettle back on. If you nip down the mini-market and get some milk, I'll have made a fresh pot of tea by the time you get back.'

As she came out of the mini-market, Beans saw Ellen standing outside the Post Office. Anxious to share her news about the weevils,

Beans called out and broke into a run – but then the person outside the Post Office turned to look and Beans' feet faltered. It wasn't Ellen; it was a sharp-faced elderly woman with a mole on her chin and dark circles under her eyes. Beans frowned and blushed. How could she have made such a stupid mistake?

'Haven't you ever been told that it's rude to stare?' the woman snapped crossly.

'Sorry!' mumbled Beans. 'I thought you were someone else!' Stumbling with embarrassment, Beans turned out of the High Street into the side road that led up the hill to her house.

As soon as she took the first step up the hill, Beans felt the prickle in the middle of her back that she always felt when she was being watched. A few steps further, and the feeling changed into a coldness on the back of her neck. She turned to look.

A large tabby cat sat at the kerb on the opposite side of the road, gazing at her with deep green eyes. It sat still, with its long tail wrapped neatly over its paws.

'Hello, puss!' said Beans. 'Haven't you ever

been told that it's rude to stare?'

When Beans talked to cats, they usually scampered off in alarm, or turned around and showed her their bottom as an insult. This cat did neither: it stayed where it was, looking straight into her eyes.

It had a wide, wise face. There was a black scar shaped like a crescent moon on one side of its nose and the edges of its ears were notched from old fights.

Beans remembered her tea and set off up the

hill once more. As soon as she moved, the cat unwound itself and walked up the side of the road, keeping pace with her. Beans got the idea that it was following her and suddenly stopped.

The cat halted at the same time, as exactly as if it had read her thoughts.

'Impossible!' muttered Beans.

She tried again – three steps, stop; three steps, stop.

Each time the cat did the same.

Beans hurried the rest of the way, but just before she ran up the steps to the front porch, she could not resist looking to see if the tabby was still with her.

It was under the tree outside the house.

Beans held up the carton of milk in her left hand.

'Is this what you're after, puss?' she called. 'Are you on the scrounge?'

The cat blinked slowly in a way that said 'no' more clearly than words could have.

It was strange, but not frightening. Beans' stomach rumbled and she went into the house to give it some breakfast so it would stay quiet.

4

Ellen's Garden

Mum dropped Beans off at Ellen's house after lunch. When Mrs Riordan, Ellen's mother, opened the door, Beans was surprised. Mrs Riordan took a lot of trouble over her appearance usually; today she looked scruffy. Her blouse was creased and her red hair looked unbrushed. Her face was pale and unhealthy looking.

'Oh, hello, Robina. Ellen's in the back garden somewhere. Do come in.'

As she closed the front door, Mrs Riordan winced and raised a hand to her head. 'Don't mind me,' she said. 'I've got a splitting headache. I've had it all day. I'm going to take some aspirin and lie down. Go on through, you know where the garden is.'

It was a long, thin garden, choked with weeds. Ellen's father joked that he liked a garden to look natural; Ellen said this was just an excuse not to do any gardening.

Beans couldn't see Ellen anywhere. She drew in a breath to shout, then remembered Mrs Riordan's headache and went searching instead.

Half-way down the garden, a strange sound made Beans stop and listen. A voice was murmuring something, so fast and so low it was like the droning of a bee. Beans frowned as she tried to make out the words.

Then she noticed Ellen, crouched on one of the branches of the tree at the bottom of the garden, holding something up to her face in both hands and muttering to it.

'Ellen?' said Beans, stepping forward. 'What are you doing up there?'

Ellen jumped, startled. What she was holding slipped out of her hands and fell to the foot of the tree. She stared at Beans with a furious expression, her lips curled back over her teeth like a snarling dog's; then the snarl turned itself into a smile.

'Robina!' she cooed. 'You did give me a fright!'

'What's this you've dropped?' laughed Beans, bending forward to retrieve the object in the grass.

'No!' Ellen called sharply. 'Don't bother with it! It's nothing!'

But her warning came too late.

It was a doll, roughly moulded from blue modelling clay. The face was just a pinch in the clay and the eyes and mouth were thumbnail marks. Two elastic bands held a piece of green material around the doll to form a dress. A long pin had been pushed straight through the doll's head and some red hair had been stuck to the top. It looked horrible, but fascinating at the same time.

'What is it?' asked Beans, as Ellen dropped to the grass.

'Oh, I got bored and decided to play a game,' Ellen replied casually.

'What game?'

'Just making up a story,' said Ellen. 'Can I have it back?'

She held out her hand. Beans looked up and saw that even though Ellen's mouth was smiling, her eyes looked annoyed.

'Why has it got a pin through its head?' Beans asked.

'That's what happened to it in the story,' shrugged Ellen. 'You can pull the pin out if it bothers you so much. I think she's had enough for now.'

'Who?'

'The doll,' smiled Ellen. 'Who else did you think?'

Beans pulled out the pin, then handed the pin and the doll to Ellen, who balanced them both on a low branch close to the trunk of the tree. When she had finished, she turned to Beans and said, 'How did you like your sour milk and weevils?'

5

Deadly Nightshade

Beans gasped. Her knees wobbled and a nasty taste came into her mouth.

'How did you know?'

'Oh!' chuckled Ellen. 'You'd be amazed at the things I know!'

'But how could you–?'

'A trick,' said Ellen. 'I played a trick on you. Didn't you think it was funny?'

Beans knew that Ellen was mocking her, but she was too stunned to mind.

'You couldn't have known!' she exclaimed. 'It's impossible!'

'Is it, now?' said Ellen and chuckled again.

Beans didn't like that chuckle: she had known Ellen for years and had never heard her laugh like that before. Her eyes were different too – Ellen's eyes were usually bright, ready to laugh at the slightest excuse; now they were dark and secretive.

'You do look stupid standing there with your mouth open like that,' said Ellen. 'Let's go for a walk.'

The garden gate opened out on to country-side. A footpath ran down to a shallow valley, where there was an old church and a clump of oak trees. Over the tops of the trees there was a view of the sea and a big cargo boat sliding quietly along.

Ellen set off down the footpath at a brisk rate with Beans stumbling along beside her. She didn't speak until she reached the low wall that ran around the churchyard, then she smiled at Beans and said, 'Will you do me a favour?'

'What?'

'There's something in there that I want,' said Ellen, pointing to the churchyard. 'It's only a plant. It's growing next to the third headstone on the left as you walk up the path. You can't miss it. It's got purple flowers with yellow spikes in the middle.'

'Why can't you get it yourself?' Beans demanded.

Ellen grew offended. 'It's only a weed!' she snapped. 'You won't get into any trouble! I thought you were supposed to be my friend!'

'All right!' Beans sighed, anxious to avoid a row. 'There's no need to get your knickers in a twist about it!'

The plant was where Ellen had said it would be. The gravestone was tilted on one side and so weathered that it was impossible to read the inscription. The plant was Deadly Nightshade. Beans remembered her dad pointing it out to her when she was little and telling her that she must never eat the berries on it, no matter how pretty they looked. She glanced back at Ellen, wondering if it was all some practical joke, but Ellen waved impatiently at her in a gesture that said 'get a move on'.

A stalk of the plant came up with a bit of broken root and a small shower of earth that rattled over Beans's trainers. She walked back to the churchyard gate feeling ridiculous and guilty.

Ellen snatched the plant and gazed at it tenderly. 'Beautiful lady!' she cooed.

'What do you want it for, anyway?' asked Beans.

Ellen glared at her. 'You're not to tell

anyone about this!' she hissed. 'About the plant or the tricks or anything! Understand?'

'Why are you so –' began Beans.

'Let's get back to the garden,' Ellen interrupted. 'I've got to put this somewhere safe.'

All the way along the path, Beans felt confused and miserable. Why was Ellen being so moody? What had happened to the Ellen who clowned around and cracked silly jokes? It was all a puzzle.

When they returned to the garden, Ellen put the Deadly Nightshade in a thick clump of weeds where it could not be seen.

'That stuff's poisonous, Ellen!' said Beans. 'It's dangerous!'

'Only to fools who meddle and don't know what they're about,' replied Ellen.

'But why do you –?'

'Hello there!' called a voice.

Mrs Riordan stood at the far end of the garden holding a tray of soft drinks. Beans could hear the faint chinking of ice in the glasses.

'I thought you two would want cooling down!' Mrs Riordan said.

'How's the headache, Mum?' Ellen called back.

'Oh, gone! It just went all of a sudden, not long after Robina arrived.'

Ellen looked at Beans and smiled strangely.

'Well, well, Robina!' she said softly. 'You must have worked some magic.'

Beans woke herself in the middle of the night by getting out of bed and walking across the bedroom. She was fuddled and sleepy, but it had suddenly become important that she should get up and brush her hair. Although the bedroom was in darkness, she had no trouble in finding the hairbrush where she had left it on the dressing-table. Her right hand came up and dragged the brush through her hair several times. Then, still holding the brush, she walked aross to her window and drew back the curtains.

The garden was filled with moonlight. Ellen was standing on the patio, looking up. She was smiling, her teeth white with the moon.

Beans opened the window and held the brush out as far as she could reach. A night

breeze made the strands of hair caught in the bristles twitch like insects' legs.

Still smiling, Ellen rose into the air, as slowly and silently as a balloon. Her hair streamed and the long black nightgown she was wearing billowed around her legs. She stepped outside the window and gently took the hairbrush from Beans' hand.

'You're dreaming,' she said in a syrupy voice. 'You must close the window, shut the curtains and go back to bed. It's a silly dream, that's all. When you wake up in the morning, you won't remember anything about it, will you?'

Beans heard her own voice, coming from what seemed a long way off.

'No.'

'It's just a silly dream,' said Ellen, and then she turned in the air and glided away, the hem of her nightgown rippling so that it made a quiet fluttering sound.

6

A Little Chat

Mum looked up and frowned as Beans came into the kitchen.

'You look like you've been dragged through a hedge backwards!' she exclaimed. 'Have you decided to go punk on us?'

Beans blushed, ran a hand through her untidy hair and scowled. 'I can't find my hairbrush! I'm sure I put it on the dressing-table last night. I've spent ages looking for it!'

'Maybe the fairies took it while you were sleeping!' joked Mum.

Beans frowned – the joke reminded her of something and she struggled to remember what.

'If your face stays like that, we'll never get you married off!' Mum said.

She poured tea into Beans' hippo mug, then added milk after smelling the jug carefully. 'I'm seeing the bank manager this morning,' she told Beans.

'Bo-ring!'

'Well, if you're going to stay in, why don't you ring Ellen up and ask her over? She could stay to lunch.'

'No thanks,' said Beans unenthusiastically.

'You two had a row?'

'Sort of.'

Mum held out the mug of tea, but just as Beans was closing her fingers around it, an agonising pain shot through her arm. It was like a hot wire running from her elbow down into her fingers. Beans cried out and the mug fell, smashing into pieces on the kitchen tiles.

'Robina!' Mum snapped. 'What do you think you're playing at?'

'My arm hurt!' Beans protested. She cradled the arm with her left hand and winced. 'It's got pins and needles in it now!'

'You must have been lying on it in the night,' said Mum. She sighed at the mess on the floor, then her crossness faded and she ruffled Beans' hair. 'Poor love! That was your favourite mug, wasn't it? You've had it since you were little.'

Beans nodded glumly.

'Tell you what,' said Mum, 'I'll nip into the China Shop and get you a new one. I might even find another hippo.'

'No, cats!' said Beans. 'I want a mug with cats on it!'

As soon as she spoke, she wondered what on earth had made her say it.

Half an hour after Mum went out, Beans had a bad attack of boredom. She had finished all her library books, there was nothing but junk on television and her un-favourite DJ was in charge of Radio One. Local radio was broadcasting a documentary about canal building.

Beans wandered from room to room feeling stuffy and shut in. Deciding that what she really needed was some fresh air, she opened the back door and stepped out into the garden.

Overhead, the washing line carried an embarrassing display of knickers and socks. Beans skipped up the steps to the lawn, sat cross-legged on the grass and looked for daisies to make a chain. There weren't enough, so she lay on her stomach to inspect a patch of clover, hoping to find a lucky, four-leafed kind.

As soon as she stretched out, she noticed the eyes: two pairs of eyes were staring at her from the leafy shadows of a rose bush, where two cats sat, patient and still.

One cat was black, glossy as wet paint and had eyes the colour of golden syrup. The other was long-haired, black and white and had green eyes; its paws were white, as though it had recently dipped them in cream. The black cat was beautiful and looked proud. When it saw that Beans was admiring it, it stood up and took a step forward.

'Nyo!' called the black and white cat.

The black cat flicked its ears and stopped.

'Where have you two come from?' Beans asked. 'Are you keeping an eye on me or something?'

The black cat started to chatter: it miaowed, peeped, chirruped and growled for an astonishingly long time. Beans was so convinced that it was talking to her, she laughed out loud.

'Sorry, moggie!' she giggled. 'We don't do Cat at our school!'

At that moment, the phone rang. Beans

hurried to answer it, but as soon as the voice on the other end said, 'Good morning, I represent the Easy Window double-glazing company,' Beans said, 'Sorry, not interested!' and replaced the receiver, the way Mum had told her.

When she went back into the garden, the cats had gone.

'I wonder what cats would say if they really could talk?' she mused.

Three pairs of eyes watched Beans as she spoke, but she didn't know they were there.

Beans was upstairs, leafing through an old annual when the doorbell rang. She was only reading it for the sake of something to do, but she still resented the interruption. It was probably the Easy Window Company again, Beans thought bitterly; double-glazing sales-people did not appear to understand the word 'no'.

There was an old woman on the doorstep. She was wearing a pink bomber jacket, jeans and trainers and the clothes did not suit her wrinkled skin and grey hair.

'Yes?' said Beans.

'You don't remember me, do you?' smiled
the old woman. 'You don't know who I am,
but I know who you are, Robina. I think you
and I ought to have a chat.'

Convinced that the old woman was more
than a bit mad, Beans closed the front door a
little.

'A chat about what?' she asked politely.

The old woman giggled at some secret joke. 'This is hardly the place for a talk. Aren't you going to invite me in?'

Beans felt a panic twitching in her stomach. Suddenly, she did remember the woman – she was the one who had been outside the Post Office the previous morning.

'I'm sorry,' Beans said firmly. 'My parents told me never to let strangers into the house. If you come back later, my mother will be –'

'Oh, but I'm not a stranger!' the old woman insisted. 'And what I want to talk to you about is rather important.' She casually pushed her right hand into the pocket of the bomber jacket. 'It's about the pain in your arm, you see . . .'

As she spoke, Beans felt an agonising searing in her right arm. It was so sudden that she staggered away from the door as though she had been struck. The door swung wide and the old woman stepped over the threshold, closing the door behind her.

'Who are you?' gasped Beans, as the pain in her arm disappeared. 'What do you want?'

The old woman's face began to ripple and smooth itself, like clay being moulded by invisible hands. The silver ebbed away from her hair.

Slowly, she changed into Ellen; not the Ellen Beans knew, but a girl with scornful eyes and a thin-lipped smile.

'What do you want?' cried Beans.

'I told you yesterday not to say anything about me,' said Ellen. 'I want to make it quite clear what will happen to you if you do. Look at this!'

She took a doll from her pocket and held it up so that Beans could see it. It was similar to the doll Beans had picked up in Ellen's garden, except that it was wrapped in red cloth and its hair was the same colour as Beans'.

'See the two holes in its arm?' asked Ellen. 'That's where I stuck a pin in. If I stick a pin through its head, your head will hurt. If I break one of its legs, your leg will break. Whatever happens to this doll will happen to you.'

'What do you want?' Beans repeated.

'I want you to keep quiet about me, and I may want you to help me sometimes, like you did yesterday.'

'I don't understand what's happening!' sobbed Beans.

'It doesn't matter whether you understand or not,' said Ellen. 'As long as you do what I tell you.' Her thin lips twisted into a cruel smile. 'Just imagine what would happen to you if I broke the doll into pieces, or threw it into a fire . . .'

'You're not Ellen any more!' whispered Beans. 'Who are you? What are you?'

Ellen laughed and shook her head 'That's none of your concern, child!' she said. 'All you need to know is that I have the doll. Just think about that.'

She opened the front door and left without looking back.

Beans slumped to her knees in the hallway and burst into tears.

7

The Watchers

Sleep would not come to Beans that night. Every time she started to doze off, she saw Ellen's face changing and the ghastly doll and they frightened her awake. The dark did not feel safe any more, so Beans kept her bedside lamp on.

As soon as she had come in, Mum had noticed that Beans was upset about something. Too terrified to tell the truth, Beans had lied miserably and said that she didn't feel very well.

If only the truth were that simple! Something awful had happened to Ellen – something Beans didn't understand – and now other awful things were going to happen, things Bean didn't even dare to think about. The summer had suddenly turned into a waking nightmare.

A howl from outside turned into ice on Beans' skin. It was an unearthly sound, a long, singing growl that throbbed and throbbed, demanding attention. Something wanted Beans to look out of her window. She wanted to dive under the duvet and push her fingers into her ears, but she didn't dare; it might be Ellen and the doll outside. She knelt up in bed and peered through a gap in the curtains.

It was another clear, hard night, with a bright moon and stars. Everything in the garden looked grey and silver: the stands of beans, the rose bushes and the three cats sitting in the centre of the patio. Beans recognised all three – the tabby cat on the right, the black cat on the left, the black and white cat in the middle. Their eyes stared straight at her, knowing she was there. The tabby opened its mouth wide and growled, like a cat used to getting what it wanted; and it wanted Beans to come outside.

'N-O-O-W!' it sang. 'N-O-O-W!'

Beans whimpered, afraid of what would happen if she obeyed the summons and even more afraid of what might happen if she didn't. Reluctantly, she put on her slippers and dressing-gown and crept quietly out of her room. The dark staircase bristled with all the horrors Beans could invent. Every bad dream she had ever had seemed to be lying in wait for her downstairs, so that the walk through the house was the bravest thing she had ever done. The top bolt on the back door was stiff and opened with a loud clatter. Beans paused for a moment, half-fearing and half-hoping that the noise had woken her parents, but no familiar voices came. It was a warm night, but Beans was shaking as she stepped outside.

The cats were still sitting in the same position. Beans climbed up on to the patio, wondering what was going to happen next.

The black cat unwound itself and paced towards her, while the other two cats whirred and popped and mewed and made friendly noises. As the black cat approached, Beans could see that it was carrying something in its mouth. Moonlight flashed on metal as the cat opened its jaws and something fell to the ground. The cat turned around swiftly and smoothly and rejoined its companions.

Beans bent down and picked up the object the black cat had dropped. As soon as she touched it, the cats purred ecstatically.

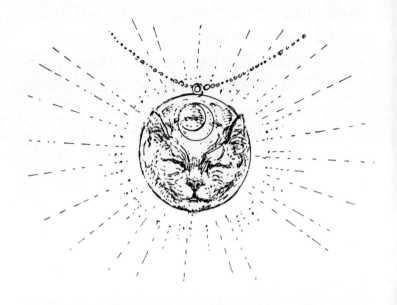

At first, Beans thought it was a small piece of moon because it was cold, white and shiny. Then she saw it was a medallion threaded on a chain. It was no bigger than her thumbnail, but it had been finely moulded into the shape of a cat's face. The cat's eyes were closed and a tiny crescent moon rested on its forehead. It was such a peaceful-looking face that some of the peacefulness went into Beans through her fingers and made her fear stand still. Almost without thinking, she ducked her head through the chain and let the medallion fall on to her chest. She had expected it to feel cold, but it was oddly warm.

The three cats stopped purring and appeared to relax. The black and white cat settled on to all fours, the black cat raised a paw and rubbed its whiskers. Only the tabby cat still stared at her.

And then, to Beans' amazement, the tabby spoke. It didn't purr, or growl, or howl – it spoke clearly in a deep, rich voice.

'Now then,' it said, 'it seems to us that you have a rather serious problem.'

8

A Talk in the Garden

'You can talk!' gasped Beans.

'I've always been able to talk,' said the tabby. 'Now you're wearing the emblem, you can understand.'

'You mean this?' said Beans, fingering the medallion. 'How can this make me understand you?'

'The emblem is magic. In fact, there seems to be a lot of magic happening at the moment and this isn't the right place for it.'

'Oh, get on with it!' sighed the black cat in a musical female voice. 'I'm getting twitchy out here in the open! Just tell the girl about Malessina and have done with it!'

The black cat and the tabby began to argue fiercely, mentioning words and names that only confused Beans more deeply than she already was. The black and white cat stood up and ambled over.

'Don't mind them, my dear,' it said. 'They can never agree on anything. It comes of being in love, you see.' The black and white cat had the voice of a kindly and incredibly ancient great aunt. 'Allow me to introduce myself. My name is Noldy. The tabby is Primo and the black cat is Solo. Solo makes such an elegant cat, don't you think? Such poise! Being a cat quite suits her!'

'You mean,' Beans said slowly, 'she's not usually a cat?'

'Goodness me, no!' cried Noldy. 'We none of us are! All this cat shenanigans is Malessina's doing.'

'Who's Malessina?' asked Beans.

Solo arched her back and snarled, 'Malessina is the most underhanded, sly, lying, wicked little—'

'Witch!' interrupted Noldy hastily. 'Malessina is a witch. Well, we all are, of course!'

Beans' head swam.

'I don't believe this,' she murmured.

'Confidentially, my dear,' said Noldy, 'I wouldn't waste time trying. If I were you, I'd just get on with it, sort of thing!'

'But, there are no witches!' protested Beans. 'They're just nasty old women in fairy tales!'

'Oh, dear!' Noldy sighed. 'I can see why Malessina chose this world! Primo, I think you ought to tell the tale. You're good with words.'

Primo seemed pleased by this compliment, but Solo was furious.

'Just tell her about jumping and let's try to get out of here!' she hissed.

'Solo,' Noldy said severely, 'do be sensible, kind gel and shut up! Primo, you may begin.'

'There was once—' said Primo.

'I think, perhaps, you should exclude the part about the Black Crab of Skar Leith,' said Noldy. 'A little too sensational for a young gel!'

'Very well, Noldy,' Primo sighed. 'There was once . . .'

Noldy had been right about Primo being good with words. As he spoke, Beans could see the places he described: the great forest that flowed over hills and into valleys like a sea, the villages like islands in that sea and the great castles with high towers and rippling banners.

In one of the castles, two orphaned girls had grown up. They were twins, but they were not identical; Solo had dark hair and Malessina's

hair was silvery blonde. Their father's sister, Noldy, brought them up and she did not have the easiest of jobs, because both children were mischievous and delighted in playing tricks.

Solo made people laugh with the blue frogs and coloured rain she could make out of the air. Malessina liked frightening people and made enormous spiders that talked and peculiar creatures with bristles and sharp teeth. When they were old enough to understand, Noldy explained that the tricks were magic.

The twins had inherited a great deal of magic from their father's will and it had been his wish that they should use their inheritance to do good. To be a witch, Noldy told them, was a great honour. Solo and Malessina began to study magic seriously, spending hours in the library reading fat books of spells. Solo gave up her childish tricks` and looked forward to the day when she could use magic to help people. Malessina despised the idea of using her magic for the benefit of anybody but herself; and late at night, while the castle slept, she went to the library to study the thin, dusty book she had discovered accidentally one afternoon. It was a Book of Shadows and the spells in it had been forbidden for so long that nearly everybody had forgotten that they existed.

The book told her how to jump her spirit into any animal or person she chose, though it was a dangerous business. One night, Malessina wandered out into the forest, found an old, deserted cottage where no one would look for her and jumped herself into a bear. She spent a fine night lumbering about, searching

for things to eat; but while her spirit was inside the bear, the bear's spirit was inside her, and when she returned to herself at dawn, she found herself crawling around on all fours, her knees skinned and her fingernails broken and bleeding.

After that, she was more careful, but she went on jumping, learning how to jump through time and between worlds in time.

She might have gone on practising her dark magic without anyone knowing, had not

Primo turned up at the castle one day. His horse had cast a shoe and he had come to the castle for help. He was handsome, rich in magic and as soon as he set eyes on Solo it was love at first sight for both of them.

Unfortunately, it was love at first sight for Malessina too.

Her jealousy was enormous: just seeing Primo and Solo together made her sick with hatred. She spent more and more time in the cottage in the forest, plotting revenge until her mind grew more and more twisted.

And then, one day . . .

9

The Trap

'And then one day she jumped here and brought us with her,' Primo concluded. 'One moment we were laughing over supper, the next thing we knew we were wild cats howling in a wood. Malessina jumped into a cat as well. She ran off and left us and—'

'She was a ginger cat, wasn't she?' Beans asked excitedly.

'A loathsome thing!' said Solo distastefully. 'Filthy fur, ragged ears—Malessina always did have poor taste!'

Beans heard nothing of this, because she understood at last why her best friend was behaving so strangely.

'She jumped into Ellen!' she cried.

'Precisely, dear child!' said Noldy. 'That wicked gel's spirit is inside your friend!'

'Then . . . where's Ellen?' frowned Beans.

'Inside the ginger cat!' sighed Noldy. 'Malessina is in your friend, your friend is in the ginger cat and the ginger cat is in our world, inside Malessina! It's going to be quite a job putting it all right!'

'Can't you use your magic?' Beans asked.

The three cats shifted their paws uncomfortably.

'I'm afraid Malessina has outdone us,' Noldy confessed. 'We're held here, locked out of our rightful world, so to speak. Being cats has weakened our magic. But if someone were to go into our world and find Malessina's Book of Shadows . . .'

'Who?' asked Beans. She noticed, suddenly, that the cats were staring at her meaningfully. 'Me?' she gasped. 'You can't mean me!'

'Listen, child,' said Primo. 'Malessina will find us sooner or later and get rid of us. After that, she'll have this world all to herself and who knows what damage she'll do! People here don't even believe in magic, so no one will suspect what she's up to!'

'Ellen!' said Beans. 'What will happen to Ellen?'

'If your friend is lucky,' Solo replied, 'Malessina will destroy her. If she's not lucky, she'll stay in cat form until she loses her mind, or dies, or both. You understand what's happened to your friend, she knows nothing.'

Beans remembered the ginger cat, pacing up and down the patio. It had been Ellen, begging for help. And Beans had ignored her and gone back to sleep.

'I've got to help Ellen,' Beans said. 'Tell me what do do!'

'Find Malessina's cottage!' hissed Primo. 'The emblem will help you. It will go cold when you take the wrong path. Find the Book of Shadows and open it to the seventh page, where the heart of its power lies. Tear out the page and destroy it.'

'How?'

'Burn it!' cried Primo. 'Bury it! Throw it into a stream! Cast it to the four winds!'

'Ignorant boy!' scolded Noldy. 'It won't be as easy as that! This is a Book of Shadows, not a child's picture book!' she turned to Beans. 'It will know why you have come. It will try to hide. It will disguise itself.'

'Then how can I find it?' moaned Beans.

'The emblem will help you,' said Noldy. 'Most of the magic we have left is bound into it. Without it, we can't send you into our world.'

'That's enough talking!' screeched Solo. 'We must send her now!'

'Are you ready, child?' asked Noldy.

'Yes,' said Beans, though she didn't feel ready.

'I think we can do it without bumping you into a house,' said Noldy. 'Houses can be tricky things, you know!'

The cats arranged themselves into a triangle. Beans stood in the centre of the triangle feeling nervous. She had always thought that the making of magic involved bubbling cauldrons and the chanting of strange words. She wanted to ask what was going to happen and what it would feel like, but she sensed that it was no time for questions.

The cats sat very still with their eyes closed and their stillness fell over the whole garden. There was a quiet that was the beginning of the magic. A breeze cold as air from a fridge blew into Beans's face and prickled her skin like needles of icy water. The emblem began to

sing and light streamed out of it, making the cats' fur gleam. The breeze rose to a wind that lifted Beans' hair. Although she was standing still, it felt as though she were gently moving; it was the same feeling as when a train pulled away from a platform.

Then, just as the moving feeling was getting faster and the singing growing louder, Beans saw something glide across the face of the moon.

'Look out!' she cried.

Ellen dropped slowly down from the sky like a huge, black snowflake.

'Noldy!' screamed Solo.

'Whatever happens, hold the spell!' shouted Noldy.

Ellen's bare feet touched the concrete of the patio and she landed in a final swirl of nightgown. There was a triumphant light in her eyes.

'You fools!' she screeched. 'Didn't you think I knew you would try this? You've fallen straight into my trap. Once I take the emblem, I'll be able to destroy you at my leisure!' She turned to Beans. 'I've finished with you, child!

I only needed you as bait to attract these three. Now I've got what I want, I shall cut your doll into little pieces, bit by bit!'

'She's breaking the spell!' gasped Primo.

'I'm going to snap your precious spell like an icicle!' Ellen gloated. She raised her left hand and spread her fingers.

Something hurtled out of the darkness, wailing with hatred. A red-brown blur streaked through the air and landed on Ellen's face in a wriggling bundle of ginger fur, biting teeth and slashing claws.

Beans cried out as she recognised the ginger cat and realised that the real Ellen inside it was not going to give up without a fight.

There was the sound of a muffled cry. Malessina-Ellen tore the cat from her face and flung it straight at Beans. Her concentration had been broken for no more than a few seconds, but it was enough. The emblem blazed, dazzling as the sun. The glare swallowed Beans and the tumbling body of the ginger cat, shrank to a pinpoint and vanished.

Beans was falling into blackness. She didn't

know if she was falling up or down—there didn't seem to be an up or down, just herself, the light of the emblem and the darkness.

It was alarming at first, but Beans slowly got used to it. She had curled herself into such a tight ball that her arms and legs were aching. Cautiously, Beans unclenched herself. She held her hand out to see what the darkness felt like, but the light from the emblem surrounded her fingers, curling and coiling on itself like ink dropped in water.

Beans craned her neck to see how the rest of her looked. It was quite glamorous, except that there was a bulge near her left knee that didn't seem to belong. The twirling of the light made it impossible to see properly, so Beans moved her knee slightly. It brushed against something that dragged itself up over her body; Beans got a faceful of fur and a paw pad pressed against her mouth.

'Get off!' she spluttered.

There was a twirling and a wiggling, and Beans found herself face to face with a ginger cat.

'Ellen?' said Beans.

The cat hissed, its fur standing up in spikes.

'Don't be afraid! I know it's you,' said Beans softly. She could see that the cat was terrified. 'It's going to be all right, Ellen. Listen . . .'

She tried to remember the words of Primo's story: they were wobbly at first but then suddenly Primo's deep, calm voice seemed to be speaking. At some point, the words of the story turned to pictures in her mind, then the pictures became dreams and Beans and the cat fell asleep.

10

The Forest

Beans blinked awake and found herself staring up at a blue sky through the branches of pine trees. Birds sang in the branches and the trees filled the air with their scent. Beans yawned and stretched, feeling wonderfully comfortable. The spell had deposited her in a clump of velvety moss, not far from a heap of massive, pinkish rocks. Through a gap in the trees that grew out of the rocks, Beans could see distant wooded hills.

Curiously, she dug her fingers into the moss; it felt real. There didn't seem to be anything magic about the place—Dead Man's Wood was creepier. The ginger cat was curled up beside her. When Beans moved to feel the moss, the cat woke up and started mewing impatiently.

'All right!' said Beans. 'I'm getting up!'

She clambered reluctantly to her feet and walked towards the rocks. It felt strange to be walking through a forest in her pyjamas and

dressing-grown, and Beans discovered that slippers were not the ideal footwear for scrambling over boulders. The cat managed the climb much more easily, making 'hurry up' squeaking noises.

'Don't nag!' Beans complained. 'I'm doing the best I can!'

From the top of the boulders, Beans could see out over the forest. To her left, she could just make out the walls and turrets of a castle, shining in the sun.

Beans' heart sank. The forest stretched from horizon to horizon; it might take years to find a single cottage in it. She glanced at the cat and wondered if Ellen were thinking the same thing.

'Come on, Ellen!' she said, more cheerfully than she felt. 'It's a lovely day for a stroll in the woods!'

At the foot of a long slope they came across a track that snaked off between the trees. Beans stood beside it, wondering whether to go left or right. She took two steps along the track, and the emblem went chill against her skin. Beans drew it out of her pyjamas and examined it: the silver was fogged. She remembered Primo telling her how the emblem would go cold if she took the wrong path. She pointed confidently in the opposite direction.

'That's the way!'

They walked for a long time. It grew hot, and Beans felt hungry and thirsty. Brightly-coloured birds, pecking at the side of the track, flew off as they approached. The cat chattered at them spitefully and twirled her tail.

'Language!' said Beans. 'You're not really a cat, remember?'

The track ran through a part of the forest where the trees grew so close together that the shadows of their branches made the light dusk. The cool of the shadows was welcome, but Beans was so thirsty she could think of nothing else. The cat was suffering too: it walked with its mouth open, gasping for drink.

Then, as she rounded the trunk of a gigantic tree, Beans caught sight of something that made her heart race and drove all thought of thirst from her mind.

There was a man standing at the side of a

track up ahead—a tall man, with one outstretched arm and a horrible green growth
over his face. A pair of antlers rose up from his
forehead, their points covered in tatters that
swayed in the breeze. Beans had to bite her lip
to keep from screaming—then she saw that the

man was only a stone statue and she breathed a sigh of relief. The tatters on his antlers and the growth on his face were moss. Where the bare stone showed, it was weathered and pitted. The face wore the remains of a smile.

The ginger cat trilled excitedly and went scampering off.

'Ellen?' called Beans. 'Where are you going?' She followed the cat anxiously.

A few metres away from the track, a spring bubbled up from an outcrop of rocks. The rocks were like giant steps, and on each step the water from the spring formed a shallow pool before showering down to the next step. At the base of the rocks, a stream twisted away into the darkness of the deeper forest.

The ginger cat was already crouched on the bottom step, lapping at the pool for all it was worth. Beans started to climb up on to the next step, but it was not easy: the rock was wet and her slippers would not grip. In the end, Beans took them off and climbed barefoot.

Water had never tasted so amazing; it was like drinking light. The first mouthful made Beans' thirst vanish, the mouthfuls that fol-

lowed were pure pleasure. Beans raised her head, laughing with relief and saw a strange face staring down at her from the step above.

11

Hunter

It was a boy; he might have been the same age as Beans, but it was difficult to tell because his face looked old and young at the same time. He had black curly hair, brown eyes and deeply tanned skin. His clothes looked old—his breeches were patched and there were holes in the elbows of his shirt. A bow rested on his left shoulder and there was a dagger in the belt at his waist. He saw that Beans was alarmed by his sudden appearance and laughed.

'I could've killed you back there on the track,' he said, pointing. 'Been a good shot, that—but then I am a good shot, mind. Could've got you while you was climbin' this ol' rock, look, easy as anythin'! Then, o' course, I could've crept up on you while you was drinkin' an' slit your throat smooth as butter!' He sounded cheerful about it.

'Who are you?' Beans demanded nervously.

A sly look came over the boy's face. 'You

don't catch me out like that!' he said. 'We don't go blabbin' our names round these parts! You got a witchy smell about you. Give your name to a witch an' you'll get magicked sure as sunrise, my old ma says. You call me Hunter.' He made a great effort to sound the 'H'.

'What do you want?' asked Beans.

Hunter scratched his chin in thought. 'A barrel o' gold, a proper bow an' a good sharp sword!' he announced, then added hastily, 'Please, miss!'

'I haven't got any gold!' exclaimed Beans.

'Ain't you gonna grant my wishes, then?' asked Hunter, disappointed. 'My ol' ma used to tell me that if I was a good boy, a Great Witch would give me three wishes.'

'I'm not a Great Witch,' Beans explained. 'I'm not any kind of witch!'

'Shouldn't go round smellin' o' magic then!' snapped Hunter. 'Gives folks the wrong idea! What you doin' round 'ere, anyroad?'

'I'm looking for a cottage,' said Beans. 'Only I don't know where it is.'

'Then I'm your man!' said Hunter confidently. 'Ain't nobody knows the forest like me.'

'You mean you'll help me?' Beans asked hopefully.

The sly look returned to Hunter's face.

'Maybe, maybe not,' he said. 'It sort o' depends, like.'

'On what?'

'On what's in it for me.'

Beans thought frantically. The only thing of value she had was the emblem and she couldn't possibly offer that.

'I can't give you anything, Hunter, but if you help me, I know some people who will.'

'Oh?' said Hunter suspiciously.

'Have you heard of Noldy?'

Hunter's eyes widened and when his voice came it was unsteady. 'You mean Great Witch Noldy?'

'I suppose so,' said Beans.

'Great Witch Noldy!' breathed Hunter. 'She'd give me three wishes, I'll bet!' He came out of a day-dream and smiled eagerly at Beans. 'There's plenty o' cottages in the forest—'oo lives in the one you're lookin' for?'

'Malessina,' said Beans.

Hunter went pale beneath his tan. 'That one!' he exclaimed, his voice thick with dread. 'You don't want to 'ave nothin' to do with 'er! She's a bad 'un!'

'Do you know where she lives?' insisted Beans.

Hunter was torn. He chewed the end of his

bow thoughtfully. 'You got me both ways, ain't you?' he cried. 'I gets rewarded if I do 'elp you an' Great Witch Noldy will likely strike me down with lightnin' if I don't.' He shook his head bitterly. 'Ain't got no choice, 'ave I? You'd best follow me.'

Hunter was not easy to follow. He set off rapidly, following an unmarked trail and Beans struggled to keep up with him, the ginger cat half-running and jumping at her side. Before they had gone far, Beans tripped over a stone and fell dangerously close to a clump of nettles. The ginger cat paused, mewing sympathetically, but Hunter didn't even break his stride.

'Hang on!' shouted Beans.

Hunter turned and retraced his steps. 'What's up?'

'You're going too fast!' grumbled Beans as she stood.

'We got to get there while it's light,' Hunter said seriously. 'Plenty o' wolves about 'ere. When it gets dark, they can see you, but you can't see them. Ol' man Wolf ain't fussy! If you got meat on you, 'e'll eat you, even if you are friends with a Great Witch!'

'I haven't come all this way to be eaten by a wolf!' Beans said briskly.

'Ah, you knows that,' laughed Hunter, 'but do Ol' man Wolf know it?'

The forest grew thicker as they travelled on, the trees jostling like people in a queue. They walked over stones that pressed painfully against the soles of Beans' slippers, and picked their way through marshy patches that sucked at their feet and smelled fearsome.

Deer broke from cover and went flashing through the trees as they passed; they heard wild pigs grunting and crashing through the undergrowth. All the time the emblem was warm and whenever Beans glanced down at it, its brightness gave her hope and comfort.

She needed comforting: her hunger was like an empty space inside and with each step her legs seemed to grow heavier. Her mind went blank and she trudged on, half asleep.

She came fully awake when she failed to notice that Hunter had stopped walking and she blundered straight into him. He turned round and pressed a finger to his lips.

'What is it?' whispered Beans.

'Can't rightly say! These tracks down 'ere don't seem right.'

Beans looked at the ground and saw a blur of scuffs and marks that made no sense to her.

Hunter nodded ahead to a small clearing. 'There's somethin' over there, I reckon,' he muttered. 'Keepin' down wind so's we can't smell it. Listen!' Bracken rustled and snapped. Hunter reached over his shoulder, took an arrow from the quiver at his back and notched it on to the string of the bow.

'Whatever you do for good luck down your way, I should do it now, like,' he said.

He took a step forward into the clearing and drew the bow.

There was a howl and then a wild-looking woman bounded out from behind a tree on the far side of the clearing. Her eyes were narrow slits and her fair hair was tangled with dead pine needles and bits of twig. Her clothes, once fine, were ripped and soiled. When she saw Hunter's bow, she stood still, lashing at the air with crooked fingers and hissing as she bared

her teeth.

Beans heard the ginger cat whimpering at her side, and in a sudden rush she guessed who the woman was. It was Malessina, or rather it was the real cat inside Malessina. The cat whined, as though some part of it recognised its spirit.

Hunter's bowstring twanged. The arrow thudded into the ground at cat-Malessina's feet, raising a puff of dust. Her nerve failed her and she ran, blind with panic, across the clearing and into the shadows of the far trees.

Hunter ran across to Beans, notching another arrow as he came. His breathing was shuddery. 'That was Lady Malessina 'erself!'

'I know,' said Beans.

'Whatever's got into 'er, I wonder?'

Beans laughed weakly. 'Don't ask! It's so complicated I don't understand it myself!'

12

The Book of Shadows

They reached the cottage in the weak sunlight of late afternoon. It was a neglected building: ivy covered most of the walls and there were tufts of grass growing in the rotting thatch of the roof as though the cottage were half-way through turning itself back into a part of the forest. Beans stared at the remains of a garden, long run wild. There was something familiar about an overgrown white rose bush, but she couldn't quite place it.

The windows of the cottage were like blank eyes, the doorway like a mouth. Beans thought about the mouth swallowing her and the idea made her shiver.

'You really goin' in there?' asked Hunter. He spoke softly, as though someone were listening.

'I have to,' said Beans, wishing that she didn't.

'You won't get me in there!' Hunter declared. 'Not for ten barrels o' gold! Fair stinks o' magic, that place, and bad magic at that! I've 'eard things about Lady Malessina and 'er doin's.'

'What?' quailed Beans.

'Probably better for you not to know!'

Beans rather wished Hunter had not said this.

'No,' Hunter went on, 'I'll stay out 'ere, build a fire an' keep watch.'

'What about the wolves?' asked Beans.

'Rather face a wolf than go in there. An arrow puts a wolf down, but arrows are no use against magic, good or bad.'

The emblem was restless: it was giving off heat and it was singing quietly. Beans knew that she couldn't put the moment off any longer.

'Will you wish me luck?' she said.

'You'll need more than luck where you're goin'!' replied Hunter grimly.

Beans walked across the clearing towards the door. The ginger cat padded along beside her. Its ears were flattened down against its head and its tail was held at a cautious angle.

'Thanks, Ellen!' whispered Beans. 'I didn't

want to do it all on my own!'

She leaned over and tried to stroke the cat, but she got hissed at.

'All right!' said Beans. 'No need to be so touchy!'

The door squealed on its hinges. The last of the day's light slanted in through the open doorway and cast the long shadows of Beans and the cat across the stone floor.

The interior of the cottage was a mess. A big table in the centre of the floor was piled high with books and papers. Bunches of dried plants hanging from the beams swung gently in the draught from the opened door. Dead lizards floated in dusty jars of brown liquid on shelves. The fireplace opposite the door was choked with dead ashes and bits of burnt feathers. Wind had scattered a dirty fan of fine ash over the floor. The only cheerful thing in the whole place was a small vase of wild flowers standing on one of the window ledges.

'Where do I start?' Beans whispered. She walked over to the table, ducking her head to avoid the dried plants. A thin layer of dust lay over everything on the table. Beans peered at a paper on top of a pile and saw that it was covered with scrawly writing. As she reached out to move the papers so that she could inspect the books buried beneath, Beans felt the emblem grow cold.

'Well if it's not on the table, where is it?' she said aloud.

At the sound of her voice a mouse darted out of its hiding place in a corner and flashed across the cottage for the safety of the open door. The suddenness of it made Beans cry out.

The ginger cat gave a distressed miaow.

'Some mouser you are!' Beans said.

The cat went on calling, pacing to and fro as it tried to draw Beans' attention.

'What is it, Ellen? What have you seen?'

The cat ran over to a window and stretched its paw up towards an hour-glass that stood on the window-ledge. Beans frowned; she was sure that something was different. She glanced at the other window and saw that its glass was crazed with cobwebs.

'Where did the vase of wild flowers go?' Beans murmured.

The emblem answered her in Noldy's voice. 'It will know why you have come. It will try to hide. It will disguise itself.'

Beans stared hard. There was something peculiar about the hour-glass: it was fuzzy round the edges and she could see part of the window through its wooden stand.

The emblem was singing now and glowing with heat. The cat dropped its paw and danced excitedly.

'Got you!' exclaimed Beans.

She crossed to the window and reached out her hand.

Before her horrified gaze, the hour-glass changed. It became a coiled brown snake that struck at her outstretched hand, its curved fangs dripping with venom.

The snake was so fast that Beans had no time to move, but the emblem sang loudly and enveloped her in a second skin of light. The snake closed its jaws on the light and was flung back. Beans heard the dull thud of its head against the window-frame. She had no idea how the emblem had protected her, but sensed she was safe inside the light.

The snake oozed off the window-ledge, dropped to the floor and began to slide towards the ginger cat. The cat cowered against a wall, hissing, too terrified to run.

'Ellen!' squealed Beans.

'You must pick it up!' sang the emblem.

'I can't!'

'It will strike the cat if you do not pick it up! It is not a snake, it is a book! In your hands, it will become a book!'

The snake was very close to the cat now. Beans swallowed a sob, dashed forward and grabbed at the reptile with both hands, shutting her eyes as she did so.

She had expected to feel a scaly, lunging body; instead, her fingers closed over a book. Gingerly, Beans opened her eyes.

It was ordinary looking: smaller than a school exercise book, it was bound in cracked black leather. There was no writing on the spine and the pages were dog-eared. No wonder it had lain unopened for so many years, Beans thought. It was strange that such an ugly little thing had caused so much trouble.

'The seventh page!' insisted the emblem. 'Find the seventh page!'

As soon as Beans opened the cover, the pages of the book squeezed tightly shut—she could feel them resisting her fingers. She ran a thumbnail down between the pages, managed to push her thumb between them, then forced her other thumb into the open gap. It took all her strength to wrench the book open.

The writing on the seventh page said: 'Of the return of spirits to their rightful owners.'

'Tear it out!' urged the emblem.

As the page tore, the Book of Shadows screamed hoarsely. It wrenched itself out of Beans' grasp and fell on to the floor, where it clenched up like a wounded spider. The seventh page twitched and rattled in Beans' fingers.

'Hold it tightly!' gasped the emblem. 'Find water! Find fire!'

A wind began to blow. As Beans made towards the doorway, a roaring blast of air hit her, plucking at the parchment page and making it difficult for her to walk. She gritted her teeth, leaned into the wind and struggled forward. Outside in the clearing, a fire blazed. Not far away stood Hunter, staring wide-eyed

at the glowing figure that staggered through the cottage doorway.

'Hurry!' croaked the emblem. 'Our power is growing weak!'

The light around Beans was fading and the sound of the wind was louder. She reeled towards the fire and with a wordless shout she thrust the page into its flames.

A force like a huge hand slapped her to the ground.

The fire howled, spitting sparks like a

furnace as its centre glowed white. Shadows rose from it and shrieked as they streamed up into sky. Beans saw the silhouettes of figures on horseback, creatures with bat wings, human shapes with animal heads. A black fountain reared above the clearing, swayed for a few moments and then collapsed on itself, fading into nothingness like morning mist.

The silence in the clearing was almost loud and when a branch snapped in the fire it made Beans jump. She sat up and noticed that the light of the emblem had gone.

Hunter approached her, one hand grasping the handle of his dagger.

'It's all right!' Beans called weakly. 'I'm not going to turn into anything nasty!'

'That was a proper to-do an' no mistake!' Hunter said cheerfully as he helped Beans to her feet.

'Where's the cat?' Beans asked anxiously.

The cat was sitting in the cottage doorway, washing its whiskers as calmly as if the burning of the Book of Shadows was something it saw every day. It noticed it was the centre of attention, bounded over to Beans and

Hunter and wound itself around their legs, arching its back and purring loudly.

'Funny animal!' laughed Hunter. 'That's the first time I've seen it be'ave like a real cat!'

'Me too!' said Beans, reaching out to scratch it behind the ears. It was then that she missed the weight of the emblem around her neck. Her hand flew up to her throat, but there was nothing there.

'Oh, no!' she moaned. 'How am I going to get home without it?'

13

A Forgetting

Hunter was puzzled why Beans was so upset about losing a necklace after all that she had been through. He watched her scrabbling in the grass beside the fire.

'Valuable, is it?' he asked.

'It's more than valuable!' Beans replied. 'I'll be stuck here without it! I won't be able to get back!'

'Back where?'

'I don't belong here!' Beans explained. 'I can't return to the place I came from without the emblem.'

'Long walk, is it?'

Beans groaned with frustration.

'Don't reckon you'll find it now,' said Hunter. 'It's gettin' too dark.'

Beans looked up and saw that it was already dusk. The idea of spending a night in the forest frightened her; the last of her courage drained away and she began to cry quietly. Warm tears splashed over the backs of her hands.

'My ol' ma always says no good ever comes of gettin' mixed up with witchery,' said Hunter sagely.

'Oh, knickers to your old ma!' Beans snapped through her tears.

'Knickers?' frowned Hunter. 'What's knickers?'

Before Beans was able to think of a suitable explanation, Hunter's attention was distracted. He tilted his head on one side.

'What's that I can 'ear? Sounds like singin'!'

Beans listened carefully and found that she could hear it too; the sound of a singing choir came drifting through the twilight. In the distance, gleaming points of light moved between the trees.

'What is it?' Beans asked.

'Don't rightly know! We'll find out soon enough, though! It's comin' our way!'

The lights were lanterns on the ends of poles. The poles were held aloft by a procession of singing boys. The choir marched into the clearing and filed around it, forming a ragged circle of song and light.

A lady in fine clothes rode into the circle on
the back of a dapple-grey horse whose harness
jingled with silver bells. The lady's hair was
white and her skin was wrinkled, but her dark
eyes looked young and a smile flickered at the
corners of her mouth like a moth.

Hunter sank down on to one knee, bowed
his head and as soon as the choir stopped

singing, he began to babble.

'Don't blame me, your Wonderfulness! Wasn't my idea! Tempted me, she did! I 'ad no part in it, really! I'm just a poor forest boy 'oo don't know nothin' about magic! I was afraid o' what she might do to me if I didn't do what she said—'

'You big liar!' gasped Beans. 'You did it for a barrel of gold, a bow and a sword!'

Hunter gave her a dirty look and winced.

'Shut your row!' he hissed. 'It's 'er! It's Great Witch Noldy!'

Beans gaped and took two faltering steps towards the lady on horseback.

'Noldy?' she croaked. 'But . . . how? When?'

'Just so, my dear,' said Noldy. 'We were with you all the time, you know. In the emblem. As soon as the spell was broken, we went back to ourselves.'

'How?'

Noldy gestured with a hand that was choked with flashing rings. 'Magic, my dear,' she said airily. 'So tedious to explain! Now you're not to worry! Your friend is safe in your own world. Primo and Noldy send their best wishes. They're sorry they can't be here, but they're occupied with Malessina at the moment. I've come to thank you and to send you home. You really are a very brave gel!'

'I'm not!' blushed Beans. 'I was frightened to death by the Book.'

'Goodness me!' laughed Noldy. 'Being brave doesn't mean not being frightened!' She turned to Hunter and looked severe. 'And you, boy, strike me as being a ragamuffin and a rapscallion!'

'Yes, your Witchness!' muttered Hunter.

'But you appear to have done me a favour,' continued Noldy, 'so I shall have to grant you a favour in return.'

'Three wishes?' Hunter asked eagerly.

'One wish.'

'Right!' said Hunter. 'Well, I reckons as 'ow I could really do with a—'

'Not now, impetuous youth!' rapped Noldy. 'A wish is a precious thing and not to be taken lightly. You will have to think about it for a while. You can think, I take it?'

'After a fashion, your Greatness!' mumbled Hunter.

Noldy's expression softened as she turned back to Beans. 'And I mean to grant you a favour, dear child. Yours is not a world meant for magic. Even the memory of it would disturb you. I am going to grant you a Forgetting. You will be as you were before any of this happened. Parts of it may come back to you in dreams from time to time, but you will tell yourself that they are only dreams and you will laugh about them when you wake. Now then, if you're quite ready?'

'Please, Noldy!' Beans said urgently. 'What about the cat?'

The ginger cat was brought and placed in Beans' arms, where it purred contentedly and bumped its head against her chest.

'Your witching is done, child!' Noldy said grandly. 'May it go well with you in your world!'

She raised her left hand and a bright light came out of it.

14

Epilogue

Beans made a new friend that summer: whenever she went out in the garden, a ginger cat would appear and rub itself against her legs. At first, she thought it was just another neighbourhood mog, but then, a week after it first appeared, Dad discovered that it was sleeping on some old sacks in the garden shed.

'It must be a stray,' he said. 'Poor thing's a proper bag of bones! Heaven knows what it finds to eat!'

Beans told Ellen, they both said, 'O-o-o-h!' sympathetically and set about feeding the cat in secret.

One afternoon, not long before the end of the summer holidays, Beans and Ellen sat in deckchairs on Beans' lawn and watched the ginger cat ploughing its way through a saucerful of Whiskas.

'You know, Beans,' said Ellen, 'you ought to talk your mum and dad into taking the cat in.'

'How?'

'Oh, usual sort of thing,' said Ellen. 'Ask your mum, she'll say you have to ask your dad, then when you talk to him, say, "Mum says that if you say it's all right, we can keep the cat." Works every time.'

Beans sat back in the hot sun and thought it through; it seemed a good idea.

'Cat food doesn't look too bad,' Ellen said idly. 'I wonder what it tastes like? In fact, I wonder what it feels like to be a cat?'

'Oh, Ellen!' laughed Beans. 'You do have crazy ideas sometimes!'